Scientists can reveal fingerprints by heating super glue. The fumes produced react with the water in the air and harden on fingerprints, making them visible.

Adults use Acetone or nail polish remover to remove super glue.

Super glue was originally called Eastman 910, but why? Eastman Kodak was where Harry worked, and the glue dried on the count of 9 and 10 seconds.

Super Glue Facts

A thin layer of super glue bonds or sticks better than a thick layer.

Super glue should ONLY be used by adults.

This book belongs to...

_____

_____

_____

A Super Sticky Mistake

An original concept by author Alison Donald

© Alison Donald

Illustrated by Rea Zhai

First Published in the UK in 2020 by

MAVERICK ARTS PUBLISHING LTD

Studio 11, City Business Centre, 6 Brighton Road,
Horsham, West Sussex, RH13 5BB
© Maverick Arts Publishing Limited 2020
+44 (0)1403 256941

American edition published in 2020 by Maverick Arts Publishing,
distributed in the United States and Canada by Lerner Publishing
Group Inc., 241 First Avenue North, Minneapolis, MN 55401 USA

ISBN 978-1-84886-647-8

Maverick publishing

For Gemma, of course! With all my love. A.D.

*To Carrot, Bo, Katana and Yukiga
- who taught me all about growing up. R.Z.*

distributed by **Lerner**

A SUPER STICKY MISTAKE

Written by

Alison Donald

Illustrated by

Rea Zhai

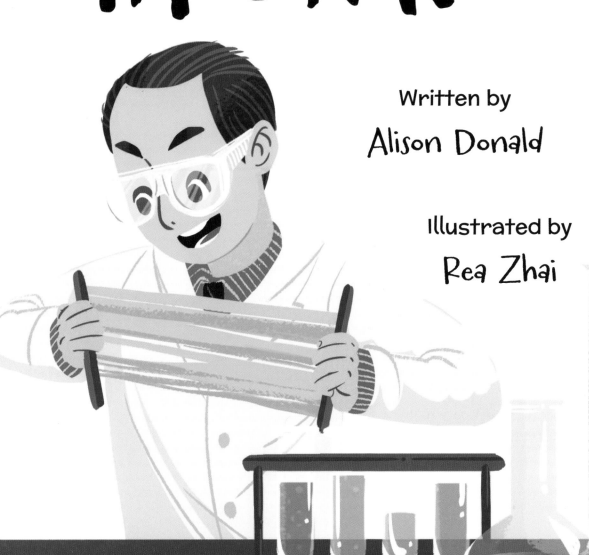

Thanks to Harry's hard work a **sticky mistake** turned into a life-saving invention.

But how?

Harry loved to learn.
Chemistry was his favorite subject of all!

...research chemist.

During World War Two, Harry was asked to develop a plastic.

It needed to be **strong, solid** and **transparent**.

Harry and his team created a mixture called:

Cy-an-o-ac-ryl-ate!

But there was a problem.

"Don't panic everyone, but this mixture is...

...a little bit **sticky.**" In fact, it was **incredibly** sticky.

Uh, boss, could you get my hand off this doorknob?

Harry and his team had made a **super sticky mistake.**

Cy-an-o-ac-ryl-ate was **not** the material they were after!

Years later, Harry had a new challenge. He needed a new compound for aircraft windshields.

Harry and his team tried hundreds of compounds.

The last compound that they made stuck the glass together.

This time, Harry put his work aside and studied
the cy-an-o... the sticky stuff.

"This sticky mess. This ooey goo. It's like a glue
but much stronger...maybe it's not just sticky stuff."

But not everyone was convinced!

So Harry worked tirelessly to perfect his new invention.

He tested the glue at home with his wife and kids.

He studied the glue at work.

Ahhh, I'm stuck!

And he **dreamed** about it at night.

Finally, after **many years** of hard work, Harry's invention was official!

Harry called it: super glue.

Super glue was like no other glue or adhesive!

Veterinarians used a variation of super glue to mend broken bones.

Super glue was used on battlefields by *medics* to stop major blood loss. A type of super glue is still used today as a first aid for minor cuts.

Detectives used super glue to collect fingerprints.

Engineers even used super glue to
fix a space shuttle
(although they were not actually supposed to!).

And to show off just how great his product was,
Harry went on live television.
"This glue works without adding heat
or pressure," said Harry.

GASP!

WOW!

At the age of 92, Harry Coover was awarded the
National Medal of Technology and Innovation
by the President of the United States.

Harry saw **value** in a sticky mess. He stuck with it and turned it into a life-saving invention. His mind was **always open** to possibilities and the world is a better place for it.

So next time you make a mistake,

what will you do?

About Harry

Everyone makes mistakes. But it takes hard work to turn a mistake into a life saving invention. Dr. Harry Coover, Jr. was known for saying that the invention of super glue was 'one moment of serendipity and ten years of hard work'.

Harry was born in Newark, Delaware, U.S.A., on March 6, 1917. When he was a teenager his car was hit by a train, which left him in a coma for six weeks! He was nursed back to health by his sisters, but having lost his memory, he had to work even harder! He later earned his Ph.D in Chemistry and then took a job as a researcher at Eastman Kodak. He rose through the ranks until he was the executive vice president for development.

Harry was awarded 460 U.S. patents. This made him one of the most prolific 20th century innovators in the chemical industry!

An iconic figure of industry and science, Harry was revered by his family and all who knew him. He is also fondly remembered by family for saying 'yaba daba do'.

A Sticky Timeline!

1917

Harry is born on March 6th, 1917 in Newark, Delaware.

1918

World War I ends.

1929

The Great Depression begins.

1939

World War II begins.

The Great Depression ends.

1942

Harry and his team try to invent plastic gun sites for World War II when they make their sticky mistake.

1944

Harry begins working at Eastman Kodak.

1945

World War II ends.